Gordimer Byrd's Reminder

Robert Weinstock

HARCOURT, INC.

Orlando   Austin   New York   San Diego   Toronto   London

Library of Congress Cataloging-in-Publication Data
Weinstock, Robert, 1967–
Gordimer Byrd's reminder/Robert Weinstock.
p. cm.
Summary: Frustrated by his failed attempts to find magic objects, a bird creates an object of his own.
[1. Birds—Fiction. 2. Magic—Fiction.] I. Title.
PZ7.W43675Go 2004
[E]—dc21 2003005047
ISBN 0-15-204903-7

First edition

H G F E D C B A

Printed in Singapore

The illustrations in this book were created in Adobe Illustrator and printed on Epson Velvet Fine paper.
The display type was set in Shaded Barnum.
The text type was set in Bodoni Book.
Color separations by Bright Arts Ltd., Hong Kong
Printed and bound by Tien Wah Press, Singapore
This book was printed on totally chlorine-free
Stora Enso Matte paper.
Production supervision by Sandra Grebenar and Pascha Gerlinger
Designed by Ivan Holmes

and
Amanda
and
Alex

The colors of late afternoon were no different than usual when
Gordimer Byrd left the thimble factory. Though Gordimer could
not remember when he'd begun working there, it had been long
enough now that he could peck perfectly spaced dimples with
his eyes closed. This made it easier for him to imagine just what
magic thing might make his life more interesting. For as sure as
sunshine leads to sunburn, Gordimer knew he was destined for
something greater than dimpling thimbles.

Gordimer's beak felt no more tender than ever when he bid
good evening to Olivia Katz.

"A delightful evening to you as well, Gordo," said Olivia, as always.

As he rounded the last hill home, dreaming of caterpillars and mixed berries, Gordimer Byrd suddenly stopped in his tracks.

There, in the middle of the path, was a magic pebble.
He knew it was magic because he had never in all his life
seen this pebble before. He could not believe his good fortune.

Gordimer got down on his wings and knees and keenly eyed
the pebble. Then lickety-split he scooped it up and flew home
as fast as his legs would carry him. Flying in a hat and
overalls is no easy feat, which is why Gordimer Byrd
usually preferred to walk.

Once home, Gordimer laid the magic pebble on a fresh napkin and held his breath for joy.

BUZZ OFF

After untold staring, he heard a faint burbling sound.
Was it the pebble? Perhaps his stomach? Gordimer Byrd
decided dinner was in order.

He assembled a quick sauté of pine nuts and squash blossoms, which he ate directly from the electric wok. Gordimer Byrd did not usually feast so handsomely, but this evening, he felt, was most unusual indeed.

Upon further examination of the pebble, Gordimer decided to put it in his mouth. Not because he was hungry. But because Gordimer Byrd knew that *having* a magic pebble was one thing. Getting the magic *out* of it was an entirely different can of worms.

He tried sucking for a while.

After delicately drying the pebble off,
he rested it on one closed eye.

Then the other.

Gordimer Byrd knew that nothing good comes from quitting
early. So he took the magic pebble in his wings and began
to rub. Upon detecting what he thought was the smell of
burning feathers, Gordimer stopped rubbing. No magic.
No burning feathers.

He tried patting the pebble.

Then humming to it.

Dancing around it.

Sprinkling it with butterfly powder.

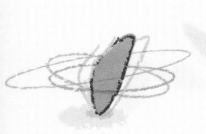

Spinning it.

Rolling it.

Throwing it against the floor.

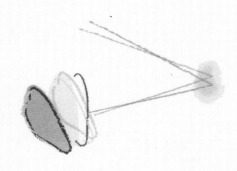

Throwing it against the wall.

Throwing it against the floor again.

This was no magic pebble, Gordimer concluded. It was just a pebble, plain and regular. And who the heck needed one of those?

He opened his only closet and shoved the pebble in with the magic twigs, the magic strings, the magic nails, the magic beans, the magic seeds, the magic coins, and all the other unmagic things he had ever found and closed the door.

Gordimer Byrd went to bed and dreamed of dimples.

The colors of morning were no different than usual when Gordimer awoke. He preened his feathers like always, fixed himself a cup of hot dandelion water and some toasted weevils, and pondered how best to tackle his weekend.

He decided to start with the closet.

The pebble was the last straw. Gordimer Byrd could no longer believe in magic things. So he set about unstuffing his closet posthaste, until all of his findings were strewn like leaves about the front yard.

After much glowering, Gordimer Byrd was visited by a
certain fancy. He decided that rather than tie everything up
for Fatback Trash 'n' Waste, he would build himself a reminder.
He was determined never to forget that magic pebbles and
magic coins are as absurd as flying people.

Gordimer worked through the night and all through the next day, piling then unpiling, tying then untying, arranging then rearranging, and so on. Now and then he stopped to snack, and to observe his progress from all sides.

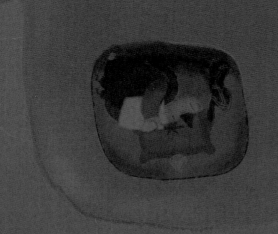

The colors of evening grew dark and mysterious. When Gordimer could no longer see up from down, he retired to his table for the night.

Monday morning arrived as it always does, and Gordimer went to work, closed his eyes, and dreamed of his reminder.

Each day Gordimer bid good evening to Olivia Katz, flew home as fast as his feet would carry him, enjoyed a quick dinner, and attended to his reminder until he could no longer see his wings before his eyes.

Come Saturday, Gordimer Byrd circled his reminder, testing the last knot of re-un-retied unmagic string with his eyes. His gaze gingerly landed on this unmagic bean or that unmagic coin, and a feeling like flying without overalls swept over him.

Gordimer spent the rest of that afternoon admiring his reminder from numerous angles, until its shadow grew too long to see.

When he awoke the next morning, Gordimer brewed some hot dandelion water and prepared to admire his reminder anew. His drink had hardly cooled before he found himself flying to fetch Olivia Katz.

After catching her breath (it was quite a long way from her place to his), Olivia Katz was tongue-tied.

"How delightful it is, and how handy you are, Gordimer Byrd," she said at last. "Why, in all my days, I do not believe I have ever seen a more delightful or curious thing."

Gordimer Byrd felt as happy as a clam sharing in Olivia's excitement—although he did not know what a clam was or why it was supposed to be happy.

He and Olivia spent the rest of the afternoon drinking tulip-bulb tea and regarding his handiwork from all sides. Then they stepped into town for dinner and a movie. Both of which, Gordimer agreed, were delightful.

VALUED CO...
OF THE WEEK

Factory Rules

NO smiling

NO skipping

NO humming

NO winking

NO sighing

NO KIDDING!

The Management

The colors of Monday morning were as different and familiar as usual, as Gordimer Byrd headed off to work, where he would close his eyes and imagine what next he might find on the long path back home.

DATE DUE

GFS Alum

GERMANTOWN FRIENDS SCHOOL
LIBRARY
5418 Germantown Ave., Philadelphia
———